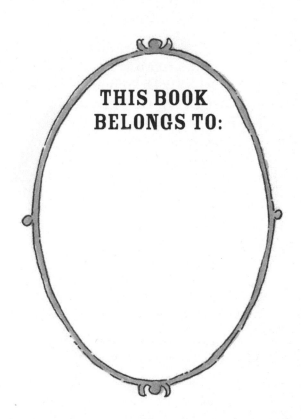

THIS BOOK
BELONGS TO:

OTHER BOOKS WRITTEN BY **KATE KLISE**
AND ILLUSTRATED BY **M. SARAH KLISE**

THREE-RING RASCALS
THE SHOW MUST GO ON!
THE CIRCUS GOES TO SEA

43 OLD CEMETERY ROAD
DYING TO MEET YOU
OVER MY DEAD BODY
TILL DEATH DO US BARK
THE PHANTOM OF THE POST OFFICE
HOLLYWOOD, DEAD AHEAD
GREETINGS FROM THE GRAVEYARD

REGARDING THE FOUNTAIN
REGARDING THE SINK
REGARDING THE TREES
REGARDING THE BATHROOMS
REGARDING THE BEES

LETTERS FROM CAMP
TRIAL BY JOURNAL

SHALL I KNIT YOU A HAT?
WHY DO YOU CRY?
IMAGINE HARRY
LITTLE RABBIT AND THE NIGHT MARE
LITTLE RABBIT AND THE MEANEST MOTHER ON EARTH
STAND STRAIGHT, ELLA KATE
GRAMMY LAMBY AND THE SECRET HANDSHAKE

BOOK 2
Three-Ring
Rascals

THE
GREATEST
STAR on EARTH

Kate
Klise

Illustrated by

M. Sarah
Klise

Algonquin Young Readers
2014

Published by
ALGONQUIN YOUNG READERS
an imprint of Algonquin Books of Chapel Hill
Post Office Box 2225
Chapel Hill, North Carolina 27515-2225

a division of
Workman Publishing
225 Varick Street
New York, New York 10014

First paperback edition, Algonquin Young Readers, August 2014.
Originally published in hardcover by Algonquin Young Readers in May 2014.
Printed in the United States of America.
Published simultaneously in Canada by
Thomas Allen & Son Limited.
Design by M. Sarah Klise.

This is a work of fiction. While, as in all fiction,
the literary perceptions and insights are based on experience,
all names, characters, places, and incidents either are
products of the author's imagination or are used fictitiously.

Library of Congress Cataloging-in-Publication Data
Klise, Kate.
The Greatest Star on Earth / Kate Klise ; illustrated by M. Sarah Klise.
pages cm.—(Three-ring rascals ; book 2)
Summary: As the performers in Sir Sidney's circus discover that friendship
and teamwork are more important than winning a trophy for The Greatest Star on
Earth, circus mice Bert and Gert write a book on how to be kind for rotten
ringmaster-in-training Barnabas Brambles to read.
ISBN 978-1-61620-245-3 (HC)
[1. Circus—Fiction.   2. Contests—Fiction.   3. Authorship—Fiction.]
I. Klise, M. Sarah, illustrator.   II. Title.
PZ7.K684Gqu 2014
[Fic]—dc23   2013044900
ISBN 978-1-61620-452-5 (PB)

10 9 8 7 6 5 4 3 2 1
First Paperback Edition

BOOK 2
Three-Ring Rascals

THE
GREATEST
STAR on EARTH

Be humble for you are made of earth.
Be noble for you are made of stars.

—Serbian proverb

➤ CHAPTER ONE ➤

Are you having a bad day?

Did you spill your milk at breakfast?

Did you trip over a dog
on the way to the bus?

Did your science project
PLOP before you could
give it to your teacher?

Don't worry. Everyone has bad days.
When you do, there's one surefire way
to improve your mood. You must go as
quickly as possible to . . .

SIR SIDNEY'S CIRCUS

⭐

*Best Circus in the
Whole Wide World*

Voted #1
by *The Circus Times*

SIR SIDNEY'S CIRCUS

⭐

ANIMALS!
ACROBATS!
AMAZING FEATS!

⭐ ⭐ ⭐

**EVERY SHOW IS GUARANTEED
TO TICKLE YOUR FUNNY BONE
AND PUT A SMILE
ON YOUR FACE.**

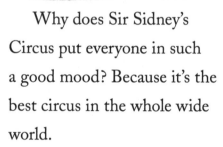

Why does Sir Sidney's Circus put everyone in such a good mood? Because it's the best circus in the whole wide world.

Sir Sidney owns the circus. He's the nicest man alive. He greets every visitor as if he were greeting an old friend.

"Welcome to my circus!" Sir Sidney says. "I'm so glad you're here. Have a seat. Would you like a glass of cold lemonade?"

Sir Sidney is nice to his performers, too. Take the Famous Flying Banana Brothers, for example. Stan and Dan Banana have been with Sir Sidney's Circus for years, often performing the same tricks. But when Sir Sidney watches them, he's always the first to stand and cheer.

When Leo the lion sings, Sir Sidney claps louder than anyone else.

And when Elsa the elephant dances, Sir Sidney places one hand over his heart and sighs.

Sir Sidney is even kind to Bert and Gert, the brother and sister mice who travel with the circus. "Help yourself to popcorn," Sir Sidney says after every show. "There's plenty for you, too, Old Coal. And Tiger, here's some milk for you."

For many years, Sir Sidney and his circus traveled around the country. They stopped in big cities, small towns, and county fairgrounds. They put on shows for fans of all ages.

Sir Sidney attended every show. He was the only boss his performers had ever known. But not long ago, Sir Sidney hired a man named Barnabas Brambles to help run the circus. Let's just say it didn't go well.

Let's just say it was a *disaster.*

It was. That's a fact.

"But here's another fact," Sir Sidney said. "Everyone deserves a second chance. We can help Mr. Brambles become a better man. Traveling with a circus is a wonderful way to learn. And just look at the cities we'll visit this week."

Sir Sidney posted the schedule.

This Week's Performances

San Diego (Monday)

Tucson (Tuesday)

Santa Fe (Wednesday)

Dallas (Thursday)

They were
all looking at the
schedule one Sunday afternoon
when Old Coal flew in the
window. The black crow
carried a letter in her beak.

"I wonder who this is
from," Sir Sidney said as he
opened the envelope. He read
the letter to his friends.

THE CIRCUS TIMES

"We cover circus news like a tent!"

2002 Bull Street   Savannah, GA 31401

Polly Pumpkinseed
Publisher

October 6

Sir Sidney
c/o Sir Sidney's Circus Train
Somewhere in the USA

Dear Sir Sidney,

Everyone knows your circus is the best circus in the world.
That's good news for you and bad news for me. I'm trying
to sell *newspapers*, Sir Sidney, and you're not giving me
anything *new* to write about!

I have an idea. I'm going to sponsor a contest. The best
performer in your circus will be named the Greatest Star
on Earth. The winner will receive a trophy.

To find out more about this exciting contest, you'll have to
read *The Circus Times*.

Good luck to all and see you soon!

Polly Pumpkinseed
Polly Pumpkinseed

P.S. I know you have many talented performers in your
circus. Unfortunately, I have only *one* trophy.

"Hmm," said Sir Sidney when he'd finished reading the letter. "I'm not sure I like the sound of this contest. I must ponder the situation." He began to pace.

Sir Sidney always paces when he ponders.

He says walking helps him think.

"But look how Sir Sidney is walking," said Elsa.

"He seems so unsteady," said Leo.

Just then Sir Sidney fell.

Oh my gosh!

He fainted!

Barnabas Brambles giggled.

"There's nothing funny about this," said Gert.

"Our friend is *hurt*," said Bert. The little mouse scurried to Sir Sidney's side. "He doesn't look so hot."

"But he's burning up," said Gert. "Look, his temperature is one hundred four degrees!"

Please, I need my doctor. Old Coal, can you find Doctor Drap?

"Aw! Aw!" answered the bird as she flew out the window.

Thirty minutes later, Dr. Dora Drap arrived.

She measured Sir Sidney's height and weight. She checked his ear wax and tested his belly button.

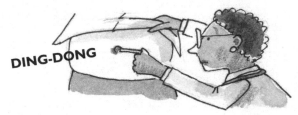

DING-DONG

Then she listened to his heart.

THUMP THUMP
THUMP THUMP
THUMP THUMP

Finally, Dr. Drap used her special magnifying camera device to take a picture of Sir Sidney's nose. "Aha!" she said. "You have a worrywart, Sir Sidney. See? It's right here." She pointed to a spot on his nose.

"What are worrywarts caused by?" asked Stan Banana.

"Where do they come from?" added Dan Banana.

Dr. Drap drew a diagram. "Worrywarts can grow anywhere on the body. A patient with a worrywart is usually nervous about something." She turned to look at Sir Sidney. "What's worrying you?"

"Polly Pumpkinseed," said Sir Sidney with a sigh. "She's sponsoring a contest to find the Greatest Star on Earth."

Dr. Drap laughed. "Why worry about that? One of your performers will surely win."

"That's just the problem," Sir Sidney said. "*Everyone* in my circus is a star, but there's only one trophy. I'm worried someone's feelings might get hurt."

Dr. Drap used her special magnifying camera device to take another picture of Sir Sidney's nose. "Just talking about this contest is making your worrywart worse. It's now half an inch wide."

That means it's doubled in size.

¼ + ¼ = ½

Did I mention my sister *loves* math?

"What should I do?" asked Sir Sidney.

"You should worry less and laugh more," said Dr. Drap. "You also need to rest. I'll write you a prescription."

From the Desk of Dr. Dora Drap

Sir Sidney must rest for one week in a quiet place.
NO worrying!

Sir Sidney studied his instructions. "I could go to my private peanut farm in Georgia and rest there," he said.

Good idea, I'll give you a ride in my plane.

"An airplane ride!" said Leo. "That'll be fun!"

"Sure will," agreed Elsa. "We'll come with you, Sir Sidney."

"No," said Dr. Drap. "Sir Sidney needs peace and quiet."

Sir Sidney turned to his friends. "We must do what the doctor says. Banana brothers, can you drive the train to all the cities on our tour this week?"

"It would be an honor," said Stan Banana.

"A privilege," said Dan Banana.

"Good," said Sir Sidney. "Now, who will be in charge when I'm gone?"

"Let me explain what your job will be," Sir Sidney said to Barnabas Brambles. "Every day you must give everyone in the circus a good meal."

"I can do that," Barnabas Brambles said. He jotted down a note to himself.

DON'T FORGET

1. Give everyone good food.

"I also want you to remember that tickets to the circus cost one dollar for adults," said Sir Sidney. "Children must always get in for free."

Barnabas Brambles wrote a second note to himself.

DON'T FORGET

1. Give everyone good food.
2. Don't get greedy.

"Here's the most important thing," said Sir Sidney. "I want you to be kind. If you forget everything else, just be kind to everyone."

"Um, er, well," Barnabas Brambles babbled. "I can *try* to do that." He added it to his list.

DON'T FORGET

1. Give everyone good food.
2. Don't get greedy.
3. Be kind.

I'll be *kind* of surprised if he can do all that.

I'll be shocked.

Sir Sidney heard the mice talking. "I want you two to be kind, too," he said gently. "Mr. Brambles might need your help this week."

"We'll be helpful," promised Gert. "Won't we, Bert?"

Bert made a noise that sounded like *harumpf.* Gert elbowed him.

"Oh, all *right*," Bert finally said. "I'll help if I *have* to."

"And hey," Barnabas Brambles said, "I'll help make sure Polly Pumpkinseed sees a terrific show. Golly, I can't *wait* to see who wins the trophy."

Sir Sidney sighed. "Someday you'll realize there are more important things in life than winning trophies."

There *are*? Like what?

But Sir Sidney couldn't answer. He looked like he might faint again.

"No more talking," said Dr. Drap. "Sir Sidney needs rest."

"Please write to me," Sir Sidney told his friends as he boarded the small plane. "Send me letters. Keep me posted on all the news."

Sir Sidney waved from the small plane. Then he stuck his head out the window and made one final request. "Please don't worry about Polly Pumpkinseed or her contest."

But it was too late. The seed had been planted. The idea was already growing like a pumpkin vine in everyone's head.

☙ CHAPTER TWO ☙

The next day was Monday. Barnabas Brambles was up early, making breakfast. The stinky smell woke Bert, who staggered out of the mouse hole, rubbing his little black eyes.

"If I didn't know better, I'd think someone was making goopy goulash," Bert said to himself. He quietly crawled up Barnabas Brambles's back to get a better look at what was simmering on the stove. He shrieked when he saw the pot of gloppy goop.

Ack! That's disgusting!

Ack! Mice are disgusting!

"Stop sneaking up on me!" Barnabas Brambles barked.

"Stop making goopy goulash!" Bert barked back. "You know everyone *hates* it. Sir Sidney said you were supposed to feed us *good* food—not this slop."

"Goulash is good enough," said Barnabas Brambles, shaking Bert off his shoulder. He turned back to the pot and began humming his favorite tune.

DA DA DUM   **DA** DA DUM   **DA** DA DUM DUM DUM

Bert brushed himself off and returned to the mouse hole. Gert was still in bed, reading.

"You know what I'm trying to say," Bert said. "Barnabas Brambles is bad to the bone. His cruelty could curdle milk. His icy heart could freeze a desert. His—" He stopped when he realized his sister wasn't listening.

Gert, do you know what Barnabas Brambles is making for breakfast? Goopy goulash!

Good gosh, that goop is *awful*!

"It should be *unlawful!*" agreed Bert. "Sir Sidney was nice enough to give Barnabas Brambles another chance. But here he is, as rotten as ever."

Gert was frowning. "Didn't Sir Sidney ask us to *help* Mr. Brambles?"

Now it was Bert's turn to frown. "I can't remember."

"You know he did," Gert replied. "We must help Barnabas Brambles, and I know just how we'll do it."

"How?" asked Bert.

Gert sat down at her desk. "We'll write a book for him with helpful hints," she said. "Go find out what Mr. Brambles likes to read."

Barnabas Brambles was still at the stove, stirring the sickening stew.

"Say," Bert began, "what's your favorite kind of book?"

"Book?" asked Barnabas Brambles.

"Yeah," said Bert. "Do you like to read mysteries or fantasies or comic books or ghost stories or biographies or—"

"Pfft," Barnabas Brambles replied. "I've never been much of a reader."

Bert raced back to the mouse hole and reported to Gert.

"He's not making this easy for us," Gert said with a heavy sigh. She was sitting in front of her typewriter. The tiny machine was a gift from Sir Sidney. Gert loved everything about the typewriter except that the *i* key stuck, making words with the letter *i* hard to read.

"It's hopeless," said Bert. "How can we make a book for a man who doesn't even *read*?"

"Easy," said Gert. She put a clean sheet of paper in the typewriter. Ten minutes later, Bert returned to the kitchen, carrying a thin book.

~27~

"*This?*" said Bert causally. "Oh nothing. Just a book we're not supposed to read."

Barnabas Brambles's reptilian eyes lit up. "Sounds interesting. Give me that thing."

"No, really," said Bert. "I don't think you should read this."

Barnabas Brambles grabbed the book from Bert's paws. "Why *shouldn't* I read it?" He turned the mouse-made book over in his hands. "Hmm, it's not very big. It doesn't have a lot of pages. I like that in a book."

He opened it and read the first chapter.

CHAPTER ONE

Do you like goopy goulash? Do you savor stinky stuff? Probably not. Most of us don't. So please don't give something to someone that you wouldn't like. This is called the Golden Goulash Rule.

Now, do you like pancakes? Probably so! Most of us do. If you would like someone to make pancakes for you, why not make pancakes for someone else? This is called the Platinum Pancake Principle. It applies not only to pancakes but to any good deed you do for someone else. Please pause to ponder before turning to the next chapter.

There was no next chapter. Gert was hoping that Barnabas Brambles would stop to think about pancakes.

"Mmmm, I'd love a big plate of pancakes," said Barnabas Brambles to himself. "Maybe I'll make pancakes for breakfast. As long as I'm making pancakes for me, I might as well make a few for everyone else."

Thirty minutes later, everyone was in the dining car, eating pancakes with warm maple syrup.

Just then Old Coal flew in the window. She was
carrying a newspaper in her beak. Elsa used her trunk to
spread out the newspaper on the table. They all read the
paper together as they ate breakfast.

THE CIRCUS TIMES

"We cover circus news like a tent!"

Monday, October 7

50 cents

Polly Pumpkinseed, Publisher
Morning Edition

· ·

Who's the Greatest Star on Earth?

Sir Sidney's Circus has many talented performers.

It's no secret that Sir Sidney's Circus is the greatest circus on Earth. But who's the greatest star on Earth?

That is precisely what Polly Pumpkinseed, publisher of this newspaper, will determine in a contest sponsored by The Circus Times.

"I plan to visit Sir Sidney's Circus sometime this week," Polly Pumpkinsed said. "I will evaluate each and every performer. Then I will decide who deserves the trophy for the Greatest Star on Earth."

Polly Pumpkinseed has seen Sir Sidney's Circus more than 200 times. "But I want to see the show one more time before I make my final decision," she said. "I want to make sure the trophy ends up in the right hands—or paws."

Good Golly, Ms. Polly!

This is Polly Pumpkinseed.

This is her, too.

Here she is again.

When Polly Pumpkinseed attends Sir Sidney's Circus this week, she might look like a woman with big hair. Or she might look like a man with a mustache. She might even look like a guy selling hot dogs.

Why does one woman need so many disguises?

"It's very important to wear a disguise when judging a contest," Polly Pumpkinseed explained in a phone interview from her home on Sunday. "I don't want the performers to know I'm in the audience until the show is over. When the show ends, I will take off my disguise and introduce myself."

When she's not busy judging competitions or publishing The Circus Times, Ms. Pumpkinseed likes to go hiking with her cat, Twinkles. "In fact," she said, "I'm leaving on a hike with Twinkles right now. When I return I will set off to see Sir Sidney's Circus. Let the contest begin to find the Greatest Star on Earth!"

Sir Sidney Needs Rest

Sir Sidney is resting at his peanut farm.

It's too bad that Sir Sidney will miss this exciting contest. But the founder and owner of Sir Sidney's Circus has a worrywart on his nose. His doctor strongly suggested that he spend the week resting at his private peanut farm in Georgia.

Who does Sir Sidney think will win the trophy for the Greatest Star on Earth? "I couldn't pick one winner," he said. "I think all my friends are stars."

❧ CHAPTER THREE ❧

On Monday night when the train pulled into the
San Diego circus grounds, a large crowd was waiting.

Are
you ready
for the
show?

Mrraare.

"We want to look spiffy tonight," Leo said. "Polly
Pumpkinseed might be in the audience."

Elsa was standing nearby, polishing her tusks. "If I
were you, I wouldn't worry about Polly Pumpkinseed,"
she said.

"Really?" replied Leo. "Why do you say that?"

"Look at me," said Elsa. "I'm bigger than the rest of you combined. Everyone knows bigger is better. So biggest must be *best*. That's why *I'm* going to win the trophy for the Greatest Star on Earth. It's only logical."

"I never thought about it like that," Leo said sadly. "I suppose you're right."

"Don't worry," said Elsa. "I'll let you look at my trophy."

"Thanks," said Leo glumly.

"Mrraare?" asked Tiger.

Okay. *You* can look at my trophy, too. Now we'd better hurry. It's almost time for the show to begin.

Barnabas Brambles had spent the past hour building a ticket booth. He was now standing behind it, selling tickets. "Step right up! Get your tickets here! One dollar for adults and one dollar for kiddies!"

Bert couldn't believe his eyes or ears. "Mr. Brambles," Bert said, standing below and waving his tiny arms. "Oh, Mr. Brambles!"

SHOWTIME
7:00

TICKETS
$1 for Adults
$1 for Children

"Huh?" said Barnabas Brambles. "What do you want?"

"You're not supposed to *sell* tickets to children," Bert said firmly.

"Is that so?" replied Barnabas Brambles. He grabbed a fistful of dollar bills from a group of children.

"Don't you *remember*?" Bert asked. "Sir Sidney said children always get in for *free*. Now you're taking money that doesn't belong to you. You're stealing from children!"

"It's easier than stealing from grown-ups," explained Barnabas Brambles.

"Oh brother," said Bert. He ran back to the mouse hole and explained the situation to Gert.

"Sounds like we need another chapter," said Gert, reaching for a clean sheet of paper.

A few minutes later, Bert was running out of the mouse hole with a fresh chapter. He found *Don't Read This Book!* in the dining car, added the new page, and then rushed back to the ticket booth.

"Hey, I was looking for that," said Barnabas Brambles when he saw Bert with the thin book. "I thought I'd lost it."

"This is the kind of book you really *should* lose," said Bert with a devilish grin. "It's no good. In fact, this book is downright *bad.* You're not even supposed to read it. See?" Bert held up the cover to remind Barnabas Brambles of the tantalizing title.

Bert pretended to resist, but he was secretly glad when Barnabas Brambles grabbed the book and read the next chapter.

CHAPTER TWO

Have you ever taken something that didn't belong to you? The truth is, most of us have done this at least once. It doesn't make you feel good, does it?

Now, have you ever given something away for free just for the fun of it? Boy, does that feel great! If you've never given something away, you should try it right now. You won't believe how good you'll feel. And here's the funny thing: The more you give, the more you'll smile. Generosity is always in style!

Barnabas Brambles stared at the children standing in front of him. A little girl in a baseball cap was raising her small hand.

"Excuse me, sir," she said quietly. "How much does one ticket cost?"

"How *much*?" snarled Barnabas Brambles.

Bert cleared his throat twice and pointed at the page Barnabas Brambles had just read.

"Oh," said Barnabas Brambles. He rubbed his chin and reread the short chapter. Then he shrugged. "Oh, let's say tonight's show is free for little girls wearing ball caps."

Barnabas Brambles laughed. "Ha! Okay. Tonight's show is free for all of you. Go find a seat." He chuckled as he watched the children run to find seats. It really *did* feel good to give away something for free.

"See?" said Bert. "The more you give, the more you smile."

"Who knew?" said Barnabas Brambles, sticking his hand into the pocket where he kept his money. It was full of dollar bills he'd collected from children. He laughed nervously. "I'd better just keep this money for myself. I'll never be able to find all the kids who paid for tickets." He stuffed the dollar bills deep inside his pocket. Then he took off his shoe and used it to stuff the dollars deeper still. Without knowing it, he was making a small hole in his pocket.

Gert arrived just in time. "What's this?" she said, tugging on a thread hanging from Barnabas Brambles's pants. The small hole in his pocket became a very large hole. Every ill-gotten dollar fell to the ground.

Good job, Gert! We'll return the money to the boys and girls during the show.

But ... but ... but.

But look! It's seven o'clock!

Barnabas Brambles walked to the center ring of the circus. He took a deep breath and spoke in a loud, clear voice. "Ladies and gentlemen, children of all ages, welcome to Sir Sidney's Circus! I will be your host for the evening. My name is Barnabas Brambles. Our first act tonight will be the Famous Flying Banana Brothers."

The audience clapped as Stan and Dan Banana appeared on the high wire. The brothers began with their potbelly-piggy-goes-to-the-parade trick.

They followed that with their laughing-leapfrog-double-loop trick.

Then came their pineapple-upside-down-cakewalk trick.

As always, they finished with their most famous and dangerous trick of all: the triple flipple combination banana-split surprise. The audience cheered with delight.

"Next," said Barnabas Brambles, "I am proud to introduce Leo the lion and his feline friend, Tiger."

The two cats—one big and one small—entered from opposite sides of the tent. They sang a funny song about cats.

Leo sang in a deep, majestic voice. He sounded like a king. Tiger sang in a high, happy voice. She sounded like a toy music box. The audience loved them both.

"And now," said Barnabas Brambles, "it is my great pleasure to introduce our final act of the evening, Elsa the elephant."

Elsa walked to the center ring. Holding a red rose in her trunk, she began to perform a slow, soulful tango. As she danced, Elsa saw a woman with an enormous hairdo enter the circus tent.

"That's the biggest hairdo I've ever seen in my life," Elsa said to herself. "It must be a wig. It must be . . . Polly Pumpkinseed!"

Elsa started to dance closer to the lady. She knew the tango by heart and could turn her wide body without losing her balance or her focus.

But that night as she turned, Elsa was distracted by a man in the audience wearing a top hat. Elsa looked more closely at the man. She noticed something dark above his mouth. "A mustache!" Elsa said to herself. "*That* must be Polly Pumpkinseed!"

Elsa began to tango toward the man. As she got closer, she turned and looked again at the lady with the big hair.

"*That* has to be Polly Pumpkinseed," Elsa whispered. But then she turned and looked again at the man with the mustache. "No, *that* is surely Polly Pumpkinseed."

Elsa turned back and forth, back and forth.

Elsa turned one more time. When she did, she wobbled and wiggled. Her tottering torso became tangled in her trunk. She lost her balance and fell flat on her belly, creating a terrible dust storm.

Elsa's friends rushed to her side.

Are you okay?

Can you stand up?

Let us help you. Does your belly hurt?

It hurts *a lot.* I'm so embarrassed. *Everyone* saw me fall. And look at all the dust I stirred up!

Barnabas Brambles tried to clear his dusty throat. "*Ahem.* Ladies and gentlemen, thank you for coming to tonight's show. Please forgive us if we end a bit early tonight."

Elsa peeked out from under her trunk to watch the audience leave. She knew she had no chance of winning the trophy now, but she wanted to find out if Polly Pumpkinseed was the lady with the big hair or the man with the mustache. Elsa waited to see which one would remove a costume. But the man with the mustache just walked out of the tent. So did the woman with the big hair. Neither was wearing a costume.

So *that* wasn't her. And neither was *that*. Ugh.

"What a night," Barnabas Brambles said when they were all back on the train. "I think I'd better write a letter to Sir Sidney and tell him what happened."

"No," said Elsa. "I should do it."

San Diego, California

October 7

Sir Sidney
Sir Sidney's Private Peanut Farm
Sidneyville, Georgia

Dear Sir Sidney,

At tonight's show, I was so busy worrying about Polly Pumpkinseed that I tripped over my trunk. Everybody saw me fall flat on my belly.

Fortunately, Polly Pumpkinseed wasn't in the audience. Unfortunately, I ruined tonight's show. I also hurt Leo's and Tiger's feelings. I definitely hurt my belly.

Sincerely sorry,

Elsa

When she had finished, Elsa gave the letter to Old Coal to deliver. Then she took a sponge bath and got ready for bed. She found Leo and Tiger waiting for her with a peanut-butter sandwich.

"Is that for me?" Elsa asked.

"Yes," said Leo. "We thought you might like a bedtime snack."

Elsa took a bite of the sandwich. "Mmmm, thank you," she said. "I'm so sorry I said I'm the Greatest Star on Earth. Clearly I'm not."

❧ CHAPTER FOUR ❧

On Tuesday morning, Barnabas Brambles was in the dining car, thinking about breakfast. "Today I'm going to make something yummy for everyone," he said.

"I can't believe it," said Gert, who was listening nearby. "He's living by the Golden Goulash Rule and the Platinum Pancake Principle."

"Great!" said Bert. "Now I can focus on winning that trophy."

"Oh Bert," said Gert gently, "I don't think you have a chance. But don't worry. I'll find a prize for you." She ran back to the mouse hole to do some research.

While Barnabas Brambles began to make scrambled eggs and raisin toast, Leo explained his theory to Elsa.

"Here's my point," said Leo, holding up a sharp claw. "The Greatest Star on Earth can't be a human. Children don't come to the circus to see *people*."

"I see your point," said Elsa. "But the Famous Flying Banana Brothers have a lot of fans."

"Yes, they do," agreed Leo. "But fans don't judge this contest. Polly Pumpkinseed does. And do you remember what kind of pet she has?"

"I don't think that means anything," Elsa replied.

"Oh, you don't?" said Leo. "Mark my words, fur is *first*. If you don't believe me, just wait and watch. Come on, Tiger. Let's practice our opera."

"*Opera?*" said Elsa. "What's an opera?"

"It's a story told in songs," said Leo. "Many operas are based on Greek mythology."

"But why are you singing an opera with Tiger?" Elsa asked Leo.

"We wanted to do something *new* tonight," explained Leo, "just in case Polly Pumpkinseed is in the audience."

Barnabas Brambles was listening to this conversation while scrambling eggs. "Remember what Sir Sidney told us," he said. "We're not supposed to worry about Polly Pumpkinseed or her contest. There are more important things in life than winning trophies."

"Name one," said Leo.

Barnabas Brambles stopped scrambling to think. "Hmm. Sir Sidney never said *what* was more important than winning a trophy. Frankly, I can't think of *anything*."

"Neither can I," said Elsa sadly. "But if I can't win the trophy, I want Leo to win."

"Mrraare?" asked Tiger.

"Of course," said Leo. "If I can't win the trophy, I want you to win, Tiger."

"And if Tiger doesn't win," said Bert, "*I'll* take the trophy."

Hundreds of people were waiting to buy tickets when the Famous Flying Banana Brothers pulled the train into Tucson.

At seven o'clock on the dot, Barnabas Brambles walked to the center ring. He took a deep breath and then spoke in a loud, clear voice. "Ladies and gentlemen, children of all ages, welcome to Sir Sidney's Circus! Tonight and every night, we begin our show with the Famous Flying Banana Brothers."

The audience gasped as Stan and Dan Banana flew through the air. They performed their potbelly-piggy-goes-to-the-parade trick,

followed by their laughing-leapfrog-double-loop trick,

and then their pineapple-upside-down-cakewalk trick.

As always, they finished with their most famous and dangerous trick of all: the triple flipple combination banana-split surprise.

"And now," said Barnabas Brambles, "I am proud to present our final act of the evening. Feast your eyes on a pair of fantastic felines named Leo and Tiger!"

The audience applauded as Leo and Tiger entered from opposite sides of the tent. Tiger began singing in her high kitty voice. She sounded like a little doll.

Leo sang in his low lion voice.

As they took turns singing the opera, Leo noticed something odd. A little voice inside his head was talking to him. "When Tiger sings, everyone smiles," the little voice said. "But when *you* sing, everyone frowns." A terrible thought began to taunt Leo.

Everyone likes Tiger better than me. Everyone thinks Tiger is a better singer. But I'm the king of the jungle! I deserve to win the trophy, not Tiger!

Mrraare mrraare mrraare Leo. Mrraare mrraare Leo. Mrraarre mrrarre Leo!

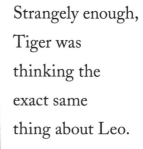

Strangely enough, Tiger was thinking the exact same thing about Leo.

And that's exactly what they did. Tiger lowered her high kitty voice and tried to sing like a lion. Leo raised his low lion voice and tried to sing like a kitty.

The results were shocking. Instantly, every pair of eyeglasses under the circus tent shattered. That's how high Leo's voice was.

Tiger's voice was so low, many people wondered if a cow with collywobbles had escaped from a nearby farm. Half of the audience ran out of the circus tent, looking for the sick animal. The other half of the audience followed to see what a cow with collywobbles looked like.

What's collywobbles?

It's a funny name for a stomachache.

Barnabas Brambles returned to the center ring. He looked around the empty tent. "Has that ever happened before?" he asked.

"Nope," said Stan Banana.

"Never," said Dan Banana.

"Leo," said Elsa quietly, "you have such a beautiful voice. What happened tonight?"

But Leo couldn't answer. Singing so high had strained his vocal cords. He had lost his voice. All he could do was shake his head sadly.

Elsa turned to Tiger. "What about you?"

The tiger-striped kitten couldn't answer, either. Singing so low had damaged her voice, too.

"I hate to keep sending Sir Sidney bad news," said Barnabas Brambles. "But I think he should know what happened tonight. Would you like me to write him a letter?"

Leo shook his head and used his tail to point to himself.

Okay. You can tell him.

That night on the train, Leo wrote a letter to Sir Sidney.

Tucson, Arizona

October 8
Sir Sidney
Sir Sidney's Private Peanut Farm
Sidneyville, Georgia

Dear Sir Sidney,

I tried so hard to win the trophy tonight. I wanted to be a big success! But the only thing I succeeded in doing was breaking a lot of glass and making a fool of myself. I'm sorry.

Love,
Leo

Tiger wrote to Sir Sidney in her own words.

Mrraare Mrraare Mrraare,

Mrraare mrraare mrraare mrraare.

Mrrare,
Tiger

Neither cat could call Old Coal, but somehow the black crow knew she was needed. She flew in the window and picked up the letters in her beak. Then she carried them through the night, using only the stars in the sky to guide her to Sir Sidney.

❧ CHAPTER FIVE ❧

On Wednesday morning, Barnabas Brambles was making French toast with sliced bananas for breakfast. As he peeled bananas, he studied his list of injured performers.

Injured
Elsa
Leo
Tiger

Then he reviewed the schedule.

This Week's Performances

~~San Diego (Monday)~~

~~Tucson (Tuesday)~~

Santa Fe (Wednesday)

Dallas (Thursday)

"We have two more cities to visit this week," said Barnabas Brambles. "And we have two Bananas left."

"Exactly," Barnabas Brambles said. "So here's what I'm thinking." He picked up a piece of chalk and explained.

"Stan will perform tonight," said Barnabas Brambles. "Dan can perform tomorrow night. This way, no matter what happens tonight, I'll still have at least one Banana left for tomorrow's show in Dallas."

The Famous Flying Banana Brothers threw back their heads and laughed.

"Impossible!" said Stan Banana.

"Unheard of!" added Dan Banana.

"Why?" asked Barnabas Brambles.

"Because we're a team," said Stan Banana.

"We always perform together," added Dan Banana.

"Really?" replied Barnabas Brambles. "So I can count on you *not* to worry about Polly Pumpkinseed or her contest?"

"*Me,* worry?" said Stan Banana. "I'd rather nap."

"Me, too," said Dan Banana. "We've been up all night driving the train from Tucson."

Barnabas Brambles sat down and looked out the window. "Santa Fe is just ten miles away. Why don't you try to get us to the circus grounds early so you can take a nap before tonight's show?"

Santa Fe
10 MILES

The Famous Flying Banana Brothers did exactly as Barnabas Brambles suggested. After pulling the train into Santa Fe, they skipped upstairs to their bunk beds on top of the train. But neither brother could sleep.

"Gee, I really want to win that trophy," Stan Banana said to himself on the top bunk. "I'm older, so it makes sense that *I* should win a trophy *first*."

Dan Banana was thinking a similar thought on the lower bunk. "Gosh, I'd like to win that trophy. My older brother gets everything. It's *my* turn to win."

There are **2** of us and only **1** trophy.

Stan and Dan Banana quietly climbed out of bed. They tiptoed to opposite sides of the train car, and each began to practice a new trick—*alone.*

"Oh, this is *good,*" Stan Banana whispered as he flung himself backward in a perfect double backflip. "When Polly Pumpkinseed sees this trick, I'm sure she'll give *me* the trophy."

Meanwhile, on the other side of the train car, Dan Banana was practicing a flying double front flip. "Hee-hee," he said to himself as he pitched himself forward and turned two complete revolutions. "How can I lose with *this* trick? I can almost smell my trophy now."

Bert had followed the Banana brothers and was standing in the middle, watching them practice.

Just then Gert scurried up to the roof of the train. She was carrying a silver cup filled with oil.

"I could tell you didn't like the laurel wreath," Gert said. "So I've brought you a different prize. In ancient Greece, winners were often given cups of olive oil."

Bert made a face. *"Olive oil?"*

"You don't like it," Gert said sadly.

"Sure, I like olive oil," Bert said. "On *pasta.*"

Gert sighed. "But it's not as good as a trophy. Is that what you're saying?"

"A trophy is a trophy," Bert explained. "Everybody in the world wants to win a trophy."

"Why?" asked Gert.

"Because if you have a trophy, the *whole world* knows you're a winner."

"Let me see what I can do," Gert said.

At seven o'clock Barnabas Brambles walked to the center ring. He took a deep breath before making his announcement. "Ladies and gentlemen, children of all ages, I have some bad news and some good news. The bad news is, many of our stars are injured. They cannot perform tonight."

"Booooooooo," the audience groaned.

"But here's the *good* news," Barnabas Brambles said quickly. "The Famous Flying Banana Brothers are going to entertain you for the *whole show!*"

"So please," said Barnabas Brambles, "put your hands together for the fabulous, the phenomenal, the freakishly fantastic Famous Flying Banana Brothers!"

The crowd went bananas as Stan and Dan Banana began to fly through the air. They flipped and dipped and practically *dripped* from the high wire.

They pranced and danced and took amazing chances on the trapeze.

The audience loved the potbelly-piggy-goes-to-the-parade trick.

Children cheered for the laughing-leapfrog-double-loop trick.

Adults adored the pineapple-upside-down-cakewalk trick.

The circus animals were enjoying the show, too.

"Wow, they're doing a terrific job tonight," Elsa said.

"This might be the Banana brothers' *best* show ever," Leo said quietly. His throat was still too sore for him to speak above a whisper.

"And look over there," said Elsa, pointing with her trunk at a man selling hot dogs.

Could that be Polly Pumpkinseed?

"That looks just like one of her disguises," Leo whispered. "I wonder who she'll give the trophy to—Stan or Dan?"

"They're both very talented," said Elsa.

"Mrraare," Tiger whispered in agreement. Her voice was still sore.

The Famous Flying Banana Brothers saw the hot dog vendor, too.

"Aha!" said Stan Banana to himself. "That must be Polly Pumpkinseed in disguise. I'm going to do my double backflip right before the last trick. Polly Pumpkinseed will see that *I* am the Greatest Star on Earth."

Dan Banana was one step behind his brother. "This is my big chance," he said to himself. "I'm going to do my flying double front flip right before the banana-split trick. Polly Pumpkinseed will be thrilled to give the trophy to *me*. Maybe I'll get a free hot dog, too."

The audience was silent as the Famous Flying Banana Brothers prepared to perform their most famous and dangerous trick of all: the triple flipple combination banana-split surprise.

Stan and Dan Banana lifted their arms in the air.

"Here goes!" said Stan Banana as he launched himself backward in a double backflip.

"Watch this!" said Dan Banana as he flung himself forward in a flying double front flip.

For the first time in their lives, the Famous Flying
Banana Brothers crashed head-on.

They fell together in a limp and mushy pile. The
animals rushed to help.

Barnabas Brambles stared at the bruised Bananas. He was too stunned to speak.

"Psst," said Bert, pulling on Barnabas Brambles's trousers. "You'd better tell the audience the show is over."

"The *what?*" asked Barnabas Brambles. "Oh. Right." He cleared his throat. "*Ahem.* Ladies and gentlemen, I hope you enjoyed tonight's show. Sorry, but we're all out of performers. Good-bye."

The disappointed crowd exited the tent. Even the man selling hot dogs left.

"I guess that wasn't Polly Pumpkinseed," said Stan Banana.

"She must be coming to the show in Dallas," said Dan Banana. "It's the only show left."

A devilish thought tiptoed into Barnabas Brambles's brain. "Polly Pumpkinseed will be at the show tomorrow night in Dallas," he said. "And all the regular performers are injured." He started to laugh in his old, evil way. "If I hum a little song and dance a little jig tomorrow night, Polly Pumpkinseed will have no choice but to name *me* the Greatest Star on Earth! *I'll* win the trophy!"

Barnabas Brambles started to hum his favorite song.

"See?" said Barnabas Brambles with outstretched arms. "*I* have talent. Why shouldn't *I* win the trophy tomorrow night?"

Just then Old Coal flew in the circus tent. She was carrying an envelope in her beak.

SIR SIDNEY'S CIRCUS

Sir Sidney
Owner and Founder
Sidneyville, GA

October 9

Sir Sidney's Circus Train
Somewhere in the USA

Dear Friends,

Thank you for your letters. I was worried that Polly Pumpkinseed's contest might lead to hurt feelings, but I had no idea how much pain it would cause.

When you finish the show in Dallas on Thursday night, will you please come get me? Old Coal knows the fastest way to my private peanut farm in Georgia. Just follow her.

Sincerely,

Sir Sidney

Sir Sidney

P.S. I don't think resting has helped my worrywart at all. In fact, I feel a bit worse. The truth is, I feel downright awfffff

"I wonder why Sir Sidney didn't finish the P.S.," said Barnabas Brambles.

"Aw! Aw!" Old Coal cried.

"What are you trying to tell us, Old Coal?" Elsa asked.

"Aw! Aw!" the crow repeated. She was using her wing to make a circular motion.

She's saying, "Follow me!" She wants us to follow her to Sir Sidney—*now*.

"But we have a show tomorrow night in Dallas," said Barnabas Brambles. "Polly Pumpkinseed will be there. As soon as she gives me the trophy, we can go to Sir Sidney's peanut farm."

"Gert," whispered Bert, "we need a new chapter for the book—fast!"

"I'm on it!" said Gert. She dashed back to the mouse hole and flung a piece of paper into the typewriter. Her paws flew across the keyboard.

Bert, who was a bit slower than his sister, arrived at the mouse hole a minute later. He read the words over Gert's shoulder.

```
              CHAPTER THREE

When in the Course of human events it
becomes necessary for one people to
```

"Gert, there's no *time* for a fancy introduction!" Bert said, shaking his head. "Can't you make this chapter short and snappy?"

"You're right," said Gert, pulling the paper out of the typewriter and inserting a clean sheet. She started again. She wrote several sentences and then stopped. "I'm too *worried* to write well!" she cried, tearing out the page and crumpling it in frustration.

"May *I* try?" asked Bert.

"Please do," said Gert. She placed another sheet of paper into the typewriter and stood up so Bert could sit at her desk.

Bert didn't know how to write a book. He wasn't sure he even knew how to type. But he had an idea. He used one claw to tap it out. "I wish the *i* key didn't stick," he said when he'd finished. "My chapter looks kind of funny."

"It's perfect!" said Gert, pulling the paper out of the typewriter. She blew on the page to dry the ink. "Can you go find the book?"

Sure! I'll meet you in the circus tent. We'll add the new chapter there.

"So you see," Barnabas Brambles was saying, "this is why we must go to Dallas. It's what Sir Sidney says in his letter he *wants* us to do. And besides, I've never won a contest or a trophy and—"

He stopped when he saw Bert holding the slim book. "Is that the book we're not supposed to read?"

"I don't know what you're talking about," said Bert.

Bert handed over the book and winked at Gert. The two mice watched nervously as Barnabas Brambles read the new chapter.

CHAPTER THREE

When in doubt, think twice and then be as nice as circus mice.

Barnabas Brambles made a sour face. "What's *that* supposed to mean?"

"It means give your plan a second thought," said Gert. "Think about what *we* would do. Would we go to Dallas and win a trophy—or would we go *immediately* to help Sir Sidney?"

Barnabas Brambles put one finger to his chin as he pondered the question.

You and Bert would go help Sir Sidney.

Righto. So what are *you* going to do? You're the boss. You have to make the decision for everyone.

Barnabas Brambles reviewed the situation out loud. "Well, Sir Sidney was certainly nice to me in my hour of need. He gave me a job. He gave me a second chance. I suppose I could give my plan a second thought."

Barnabas Brambles closed his eyes. After a minute of thinking, he finally said: "On second thought I think we should—"

CHAPTER SIX

The moon was tucked behind heavy clouds as Old Coal guided the circus train through the night. Stan and Dan Banana followed the crow's every move across New Mexico, Texas, Louisiana, Mississippi, and Alabama.

"It's so dark," said Stan Banana.

"I can't see a thing," said Dan Banana.

"Here," said Gert, holding a candle. "Does this help?"

"Yes," said Stan Banana.

"Thanks, Gert," said Dan Banana.

"Just trying to be helpful," said Gert. "Golly, I hope we get to Georgia soon. We *have* to help Sir Sidney."

"Don't worry," said Bert, bringing another candle. "I'm sure Sir Sidney is fine. When we get there, he'll probably be sitting in a chair and reading a book. We'll all have a good laugh."

But Bert was wrong.

When the train finally arrived at Sir Sidney's private peanut farm the next morning, there was nothing funny about what they found. Sir Sidney was in BIG trouble.

Is he okay?

Is he alive?

He's alive but very weak.

Look at the size of that worrywart! It's like an apricot with a polka dot!

We must call an ambulance!

~91~

"We need Sir Sidney's doctor," said Stan Banana.

"Yes," said Dan Banana. "Call Doctor Drap."

Leo dialed the number. He was so nervous, his paws were shaking. "Doctor Drap?" he said when she answered.

This is Leo the lion. Sir Sidney is sick. His worrywart is much worse. We think he ... What? Yes. Really? Good idea. Okay. We'll do that. Thank you.

Leo hung up the phone.

"What'd she say?" everyone asked.

"There's a hospital twenty miles from here," said Leo. "Doctor Drap will meet us there."

"But how will we get Sir Sidney to the hospital?" asked Elsa.

"On the train, of course!" said the Famous Flying Banana Brothers. "Come on. Let's go!"

Elsa used her trunk as a stretcher to carefully move Sir Sidney.

"Unnnnnhhhh," Sir Sidney groaned.

"Don't try to talk," said Gert. "We're taking you to a hospital."

"Unnnnnhhhh," Sir Sidney repeated.

They worked together to load Sir Sidney onto the train. Barnabas Brambles spoke quietly to the Famous Flying Banana Brothers. "Can you make this train go as fast as an ambulance?"

"We can make it go even *faster*," said Stan Banana.

"But it would be nice if we had a siren," added Dan Banana. "We should warn people to stay out of the way."

Tiger closed her eyes and began singing. Her high kitty voice sounded exactly like an ambulance siren.

MrrAAAAre
MrrAAAAre
MrrAAAAAAAAAAre

Stan and Dan Banana rocketed the train over the peanut farm. They flipped and dipped the train. They pranced and danced it, too.

MrrAAAAAAAAAre

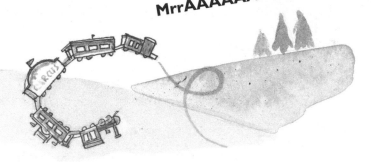

The train was traveling faster and faster.

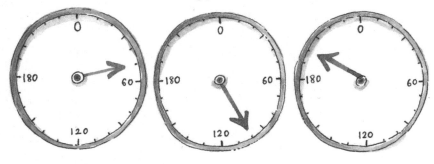

With a triple flipple combination banana-split surprise, the train landed at the hospital.

Dr. Drap was waiting for them on the second floor.
"Bring Sir Sidney up here," she called from a window.
"Quickly!"

Elsa used her trunk to lift Sir Sidney up to the
second-floor window. "Nicely done," said Dr. Drap. "I'll
take it from here."

"Can we help?" yelled Bert.

"No," said Dr. Drap. "You'll just be in the way."

In the way?" Bert repeated. "I'm only three inches tall.
Come on, Gert. We're going in."

But mice aren't allowed in hospitals. See?

NO MICE ALLOWED!

Oh yeah? Watch this.

Bert made a mad dash for the front door. To save time, he hopped onto a nurse's shoe. Gert followed right behind, riding in the cuff of a doctor's trousers.

Once inside the hospital, Bert and Gert ran up the stairs to the second floor and began looking for Sir Sidney.

"He's not here," said Gert, peeking in one room.

"Or here," said Bert from across the hall.

They searched every room. Finally, in the last room they checked, they found Sir Sidney. He was in bed. His eyes were closed. His heart was beating very quietly.

THUMP THUMP
THUMP THUMP
THUMP THUMP

Dr. Drap was writing a report about Sir Sidney's worrywart.

"Good grief," Gert whispered. "I wonder how big it is now." She scampered up the bedspread and measured Sir Sidney's worrywart. "It's exactly one inch wide."

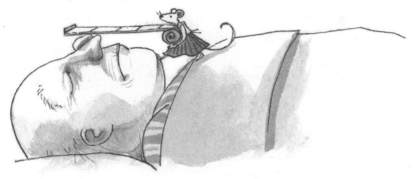

"What are *you* doing here?" Dr. Drap demanded, shaking a pen at Gert. "Mice aren't allowed in this hospital. It's against the rules!"

"Some rules were made to be broken," Bert said, racing up Dr. Drap's lab coat. He grabbed her pen and used it as a pole vault to catapult himself onto Sir Sidney's bed. He stood on Sir Sidney's chest and spoke directly to his friend. "Can you hear me, Sir Sidney? If so, please open your eyes."

"We don't want you to be sick," Gert added, her tiny eyes filling with tears. "The circus *needs* you. Isn't there *anything* we can do to make you feel better?"

Sir Sidney didn't answer. He didn't even open his eyes.

Dr. Drap looked puzzled. "I don't understand how Sir Sidney's worrywart could've grown so big when he was resting," she said. "Unless . . . "

"Unless *what*?" asked Gert.

"Unless," repeated Dr. Drap slowly, "Sir Sidney received some worrisome news this week."

Gert and Bert looked at each other. They were both thinking the same thing.

Poor Sir Sidney. We've given him *plenty* to worry about this week.

Just then, Sir Sidney's lips moved. "Shhh," he murmured.

Dr. Drap held a finger to her lips. "Shhh. He wants us to be quiet."

But Sir Sidney turned his head back and forth on the pillow. "Shhh," he said again.

"*Shhh?*" asked Bert.

Sir Sidney smiled faintly. He managed to say one word in a weak voice. "Show."

"*Show?*" said Gert. "Would you like to see a *show*, Sir Sidney?"

With great effort, Sir Sidney nodded.

Bert turned a cartwheel. "If it's a show you want, it's a show you'll get. Doctor Drap, can you help us push Sir Sidney's bed over to the window?"

"I suppose it couldn't hurt," said Dr. Drap.

Together they pushed Sir Sidney's bed across the room.

"Let's prop up his head with pillows so he can look out the window," said Gert. "Perfect. Now just sit tight, Sir Sidney. Everyone's waiting outside. They'll put on a show—just for you!"

"That's right," said Bert. "Your private circus is coming right up! Doctor Drap, you can watch, too. Today's show is free."

Dr. Drap looked at her patient. Then she looked at the two talking mice. "I suggest you hurry," she said.

🌿 CHAPTER SEVEN 🌿

Bert and Gert raced down the hallway.

"There's no time to waste," Gert said as she ran. "We'll tell everyone to get in their costumes quickly."

Immediately! The show must begin right away!

But when they got outside, they found their friends surrounded by doctors.

"What's going on?" asked Bert.

"If you're injured, please step to the back of the line," replied a busy doctor. He was wrapping bandages around the Famous Flying Banana Brothers' bruised ribs.

"Injured?" said Bert. He spoke directly to Stan and Dan Banana. "You guys have to put on a show for Sir Sidney—now!"

"We can't perform now," said Stan Banana.

"We can't even touch our toes," added Dan Banana. "The doctor says we have to rest. We must do what the doctor says."

Gert hurried over to talk to Leo.

Leo, I know your throat is sore, but can you *please* put on a show for Sir Sidney?

I'm not even supposed to be talking. Doctor's orders. Ask Sir Sidney if he can wait one day.

"Mrraaare mrraare," said Tiger in a raspy voice. She had strained her voice a second time by crying like a siren.

"The kitty's right," said a doctor who was examining Elsa's belly. "Two days would be better. Tell Sir Sidney he can see an excellent show in two days."

"And me," said Bert.

"And me," said Gert.

"Aw! Aw!" said Old Coal.

The black bird had just arrived at the windowsill.

Bert scratched his ears and looked at his sister. "Are you thinking what I'm thinking?"

"Yes," she said. "Old Coal, are you willing to help?"

"Aw!" cried the crow.

Gert turned to the Barnabas Brambles. "Can you please hum that silly tune you've been humming all week?"

"Sure!" he said.

And so Bert and Gert, along with Old Coal, put on a private show for Sir Sidney. It looked and sounded something like this . . .

(Sing to the tune of the William Tell Overture,
also known as the Lone Ranger theme song,
by G. Rossini.)

When you're sick
When you're sad
When you're feeling blue

When there's ick
And it's bad
And you think life's through

When you're down
In the dumps
And the smiles are few
Call our naaaaaaaaame! We'll be there for you!

When you're worried
And you're stressed
And you feel left out

When you're hurried
And distressed
And you want to shout

When you scurry
To be best
But you're full of doubt
Call our naaaaaaaaame! We'll be there for you!

(Refrain)
We're two mice and a crow with a show
  We hope will make the sadness go away.
We're two mice and a crow with a show
  We hope will help to save this lousy day.
We're two mice and a crow with a show
  We hope will make the badness go away.
We're two mice and a crow with a show
  who really only want to say . . .

Can Three-Ring Rascals help our friend today?
Can Three-Ring Rascals make this end okay?

(Take a deep breath and repeat
once more from the beginning.)

When they finished, everyone stared up at Sir Sidney's window.

"Did it work?" Bert asked. "Did we help?"

"Did our show make any difference at all?" Gert said with a sniffle.

At first there was no answer. Then, very faintly, they heard the sound of two hands clapping. It was Sir Sidney! He was applauding from his second-floor window.

"That," he said softly, "was a fine show."

"Fine?" yelled a woman from a third-floor window. "That was the best show I've ever seen in my whole *life*!"

"Who in the world is that?" asked Bert, looking up.

"My name is Polly Pumpkinseed," said the woman grandly.

"Polly Pumpkinseed?" everyone cried at once.

"That's me," she hollered. "I'm the publisher of the *Circus Times* and the judge of the Greatest Star on Earth contest. You probably don't recognize me because I'm not wearing a disguise."

I'm confused. What are you doing here?

See this and this?

I tripped over my cat while hiking on Sunday. I broke my leg and my arm.

"Sorry to hear that," said Barnabas Brambles. Then he thought for a moment. "Is this the *only* show you've seen this week?"

"Correct," said Polly Pumpkinseed. "I've been stuck here since Sunday."

"Mew mew," said a pumpkin-colored cat as it jumped up on the window ledge.

"As you can see," said Polly Pumpkinseed, "I brought Twinkles with me to the hospital. I brought something else, too."

She disappeared from the window for a minute. When she returned, she was holding a trophy.

"This," said Polly Pumpkinseed, "is the trophy for the Greatest Star on Earth. I'm ready to give it to the winner right now."

CHAPTER EIGHT

No one knew what to say.

"Well?" said Polly Pumpkinseed finally. "Don't you want to know who the winner is?"

"Of course," said Elsa. "But I already know who won. The trophy belongs to Bert and Gert for putting on such a terrific show for Sir Sidney."

"That's very nice of you," said Gert. "But I think the trophy belongs to the Famous Flying Banana Brothers. Because of them, we were able to get Sir Sidney to the hospital."

"Thanks," said Stan Banana. "But I think the trophy should go to Leo."

"Me, too," said Dan Banana. "Leo called Doctor Drap. Without Leo, we wouldn't have known where to take Sir Sidney."

"Thank you," said Leo. "But we couldn't have traveled

safely to the hospital without Tiger's siren. I think the trophy should go to Tiger."

"Mrraare mrraare," said Tiger, rubbing up against Elsa's trunk.

"Tiger's right," said Barnabas Brambles. "Elsa used her trunk as a stretcher to move Sir Sidney. I think Elsa should get the trophy."

"Thank you, Mr. Brambles," said Elsa. "But *you're* the one who decided to follow Old Coal to Sir Sidney's private peanut farm. I think you should get the trophy."

"Aw! Aw!" cried Old Coal as she danced in the air.

"Old Coal!" cried Gert. "How could we forget *you*?"

"You delivered our letters!" Elsa said.

"You brought us news from Sir Sidney!" Leo added.

"You put on a great show with Gert and Bert," said Stan Banana.

But the black crow shook her shiny beak in the air.

"No?" said Bert. "Then who *should* win?"

Old Coal flew up to Sir Sidney's window and grabbed a pen from Dr. Drap's pocket.

"Look," said Gert. "Old Coal is going to write us a message."

But the bird didn't write anything. Instead, she used the pen to draw a circle around two letters on the train.

"*U–S*," said Elsa.

"Us," said Leo.

"Exactly!" said Polly Pumpkinseed. She tied a rope around the trophy and lowered it out her window. "I am proud to award this trophy to *all* of you. Now hold still while I take a picture. Say *cheese*!"

"CHEESE!"

The photo ran the next day in the *Circus Times*.

THE CIRCUS TIMES

"We cover circus news like a tent!"

Friday, October 11　　　　　　　　　　　**50 cents**

Polly Pumpkinseed, Publisher
Morning Edition

. . . .

Who's the Greatest Star on Earth?
THEY Are!

Members of Sir Sidney's Circus
share a trophy.

A mouse speaks
to the crowd.

After an exciting show last night, Polly Pumpkinseed gave the prize for the Greatest Star on Earth to Sir Sidney's Circus.

"This fine circus is a marvelous example of the power of teamwork," said Ms. Pumpkinseed from the window of her hospital room. "By working together, these performers always dazzle and delight."

"We haven't been too dazzling lately," said Stan Banana.

"Or delightful," added Dan Banana.

"The truth is," said Elsa the elephant, "our shows have been pretty disappointing this week. We've all been trying to win the trophy for oursel—"

Before the elephant could finish, a mouse appeared in Polly Pumpkinseed's window. The tiny creature spoke in a breathless manner, as if he had just scampered up many flights of stairs.

"Why don't we just say thank you for this nice trophy and leave it at that?" asked the mouse.

"Nicely said," replied Polly Pumpkinseed. "Now scoot before Twinkles takes a bite out of your bottom."

Sir Sidney's Worrywart Is Gone

How do you recover from a world-class worrywart? If you're Sir Sidney, you watch the members of your circus being kind to one another.

Dr. Dora Drap was at Sir Sidney's side last night at the hospital. "When Sir Sidney saw everyone offering the trophy to someone else, his worrywart started shrinking until it went *poof* and disappeared," she said.

According to Dr. Dora Drap, worrywarts are common. "Many things can cause us to worry," she

Circus founder is cured by the kindness of friends.

said. "But a kind word or deed can do wonders. Sometimes that's all we need to feel better."

Polly Pumpkinseed Needs Rest

Some days Polly Pumpkinseed will have to exercise her leg. Other days she'll have to exercise her arm. Some days she'll have to exercise her leg and her arm if she wants to recover from her hiking mishap.

"That's fine with me," said Polly Pumpkinseed, "as long as I have a good book and my cat, Twinkles. She's my little star."

Polly Pumpkinseed also reported that sales of The Circus Times are at an all-time high. "Just goes to prove that everyone loves a contest almost as much as a circus."

Polly Pumpkinseed with her cat, Twinkles.

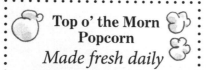

Top o' the Morn Popcorn
Made fresh daily

CHAPTER NINE

On Saturday everyone, including Sir Sidney, was back on the train.

Elsa held a hot water bottle on her sore belly. Leo and Tiger sipped tea with honey to soothe their scratchy throats. Stan and Dan Banana compared bruises.

But Sir Sidney felt strong and healthy. "I'll cook breakfast today," he said.

He made cheese omelets, hash browns, blueberry muffins, peanut-butter waffles, banana milkshakes, and freshly squeezed orange juice. Bert and Gert helped.

"This is delicious," Barnabas Brambles said. "You're really a *terrific* chef."

"Thank you," Sir Sidney said. "I hear *you* were a terrific boss this week. Was it difficult?"

"Not a bit," said Barnabas Brambles. "It's easy when you know the Golden Goulash Rule and the Platinum Pancake Principle. It's also important to remember that generosity is always in style. But the most important thing is this: When in doubt, think twice and then be as nice as circus mice. I learned all of this from—"

He stopped when he remembered that he'd learned everything from a book he wasn't supposed to read.

"Where did you say you learned all this?" Sir Sidney asked.

"Um, uh, er . . ." Barnabas Brambles babbled. "I'm not sure I should tell you."

"Please," said Sir Sidney. "I'm curious."

Barnabas Brambles handed over the book.

Sir Sidney looked at the unusual cover. Then he opened the book and read every page. When he'd finished, he bent down to look inside the mouse hole. He had a hunch Gert and Bert were inside the hole, listening.

Gert? Bert? Are you two in there?

I don't know. We *did* trick Barnabas Brambles into reading that book. Where'd you come up with all those rules, anyway?

Oh dear. Do you think Sir Sidney is mad?

Gert's eyes burned with tears. "I made it all *up*!" she squeaked. "Out of my own little head."

Bert blew out a big breath of air. "Well, there's no sense hiding from the truth. Come on. Let's see what Sir Sidney has to say."

Together, Bert and Gert walked slowly out of the mouse hole. They couldn't believe what they saw: Sir Sidney was smiling!

"This book is brilliant!" Sir Sidney said.

"Oh, I'm so relieved," said Gert, holding one paw over her heart.

"Did you really like it?" Bert asked Sir Sidney.

"I loved every word," Sir Sidney replied. "But I need to fix the *i* key on that typewriter. It doesn't work properly."

Barnabas Brambles cleared his throat. "May I suggest you leave the typewriter just as it is?"

"Why?" asked Sir Sidney.

"Because," said Barnabas Brambles, "it might be a nice reminder that even if *I* sometimes get stuck, *we* can work together just fine."

"What do you think, Gert?" asked Sir Sidney. "It's your typewriter."

She nodded her furry little head in agreement. "I think that's a *refidea*."

really + fine + idea = refidea

I bet that's good with chips and salsa.

"So you're not mad that we tricked you into reading a book?" Bert asked Barnabas Brambles.

"Or," said Gert, "that I made up the Golden Goulash Rule and the Platinum Pancake Principle?"

"Mad?" said Barnabas Brambles. "On the contrary, you helped me follow Sir Sidney's instructions." He pulled out his notes and showed them to Gert and Bert.

DON'T FORGET

1. Give everyone good food.
2. Don't get greedy.
3. Be kind.

"That last one is the hardest of all," said Barnabas Brambles. "Being kind can be tough, especially when a trophy is involved."

"We all have times when it's difficult to be kind," said Sir Sidney. "It's not easy to give up something you had your heart set on. But someday you'll learn there are more important things in this world than trophies."

Barnabas Brambles's eyes widened.

I *did* discover something this week that's more important than winning a trophy.

What?

"Helping a friend," said Barnabas Brambles.

Sir Sidney smiled. "I'm so grateful that you came to my rescue. Now, let's talk about the schedule for next week."

"We owe the people in Dallas a show," said Elsa, who never forgot a date.

"I think we owe the people in Santa Fe another show, too," said Stan Banana.

"A *better* show," added Dan Banana. "We won't crash this time."

"We should go back to all the cities we visited this week," said Leo. "I know I could do a better job."

"Me, too," said Elsa.

"Me three," said Stan Banana.

"Me four," said Dan Banana.

"Me five," said Gert.

"Mrraare mrraare," said Tiger.

"Me excited," said Bert. "I mean, *I'm* excited. Being an author is fun! Gert, will you teach me how to type?"

Sure! But first, I want to give you a silver medal for writing a terrific chapter.

Thanks.

Bert was frowning.

"*Now* what's wrong?" asked Gert.

"Nothing," muttered Bert. "It's really nice, Gert, and I appreciate it. But why silver and not gold?"

"Because," said Gert, "the top winners at the first modern Olympic Games in Athens, Greece, in 1896 were given *silver* medals. Gold was considered too precious." She paused. "Anyway, you said you wanted a quarter, remember?"

Bert looked more closely at the silver medal. It was a quarter hanging from a ribbon.

The members of Sir Sidney's Circus spent the rest of the day preparing for the busy week ahead. That night before bedtime, Sir Sidney asked everyone to look at the sky. "See all those stars?" he said softly. "Each is wonderful in its own special way."

"Like snowflakes," said Stan Banana.

"Like seashells," said Dan Banana.

"Like you and me," said Elsa, curling her trunk around Leo's shoulder.

"Like all of us!" said Bert. He had combed the fur on his head straight up so he looked like a lady with an enormous hairdo.

Everyone laughed, including Sir Sidney. Laughing made his heart beat in a happy, healthy, worry-free rhythm.

THUMP THUMP
THUMP THUMP
THUMP THUMP

After such a hard week, it felt good to laugh—not at Bert or at anyone—but at *life*. It could be so funny and surprising.

They laughed because they were happy to be together again. They laughed because they were friends. And then they laughed because they were laughing.

They knew that as long as they were friends, there would be more laughs the next day and the next day and the next day after that.

That night as they fell asleep, everyone felt very lucky
to belong to Sir Sidney's Circus.

And no one dreamed about a trophy.

Well, not much anyway.

Anybody feel like taking a cruise?

Here's a sneak peek at

≫ Three-Ring Rascals, BOOK 3: ≪

THE CIRCUS GOES TO SEA

This Way

Flora Endora Eliza LaBuena LaPasta
Aboard the SS *Spaghetti*

November 3

Sir Sidney
Owner and Founder
Sir Sidney's Circus
Somewhere in the USA

Dear Sir Sidney,

I would like to invite your circus to be my guests
aboard the SS *Spaghetti*. The *Spaghetti* is a
floating palace of elegance and entertainment.
It also happens to be my home.

I hope you can join me on the ship's next voyage.
We will depart New York City at eleven o'clock in
the morning on November 4. (That's tomorrow.)

Sincerely,

Flora Endora Eliza LaBuena LaPasta

Barnabas Brambles waved away all their concerns as if he were waving away a harmless fly. "Why are you so worried? Where's your sense of adventure?" Then he lowered his voice. "Don't you *get* it? This is the opportunity of a lifetime. Big things happen when you take a chance."

Leo looked at Barnabas Brambles.

Why are you so eager to go to sea?

Have you ever been on a ship?

Never. But ever since I was a little boy I've wanted to go to sea.

"Aw! Aw!" Old Coal cried. Barnabas Brambles laughed at the crow. "Did you think I'd forget you? No way. You're coming with us, Old Coal. We wouldn't go without our favorite fine-feathered friend."

But the crow repeated herself. "Aw! Aw!" She flew over to Sir Sidney's desk and tapped Miss LaPasta's letter with her beak.

P.S. I would prefer that Barnabas Brambles *not* join us on this voyage. I've heard he's the meanest man alive.

In an instant, Barnabas Brambles's smile turned upside down. The happiness he had felt a minute earlier was replaced by a heavy disappointment that sat like a sandbag in his stomach. He could say only one word: "Oh."

"Oh indeed," said Sir Sidney with a sigh. "I guess that settles it. We're going to sea."

"Send me a postcard," Barnabas Brambles mumbled glumly.

"That won't be necessary," said Sir Sidney. "You're coming with us."

"But Miss LaPasta doesn't want me to come," said Barnabas Brambles. "She said so in her P.S."

"I know," said Sir Sidney. "And that's exactly why you *are* coming. I want Miss Flora Endora Eliza LaBuena LaPasta to see what a fine man you're becoming. Now pack your bags, everyone. The circus is going to sea."

ABOUT THE AUTHOR AND ILLUSTRATOR

KATE KLISE and **M. SARAH KLISE** are sisters who like to write (Kate) and draw (Sarah). They began making books when they were little girls who shared a bedroom in Peoria, Illinois. Kate now lives and writes in an old farmhouse on forty acres in the Missouri Ozarks. Sarah draws and dwells in a Victorian cottage in Berkeley, California. Together the Klise sisters have created more than twenty award-winning books for young readers. Their goal always is to make the kind of fun-to-read books they loved years ago when they were kids.

To learn more about the Klise sisters, visit their website: www.kateandsarahklise.com.

You might also enjoy visiting Sir Sidney and his friends at www.threeringrascals.com.